Mystery of the
Bewitched
Bookmobile

Mystery of the
Bewitched
Bookmobile

Florence Parry Heide
and Roxanne Heide

Illustrations by Seymour Fleishman

ALBERT WHITMAN & Company
Chicago

Library of Congress Cataloging-in-Publication data

Heide, Florence Parry.
Mystery of the bewitched bookmobile / by Florence Parry Heide and Roxanne
Heide Pierce ; ill. by Seymour Fleishman.
Summary: Why would anyone break into a bookmobile
and take nothing? The Spotlight Club investigates.
ISBN 978-0-8075-4808-0
[1. Bookmobiles—Fiction. 2. Mystery and detective stories] I. Pierce, Roxanne Heide,
joint author. II. Fleishman, Seymour, illustrator. III. Title.
PZ7.H36Mye
[Fic]
75-6763

Printed in the United States of America.

10 9 8 7 6 5 4 3 2 1 LB 16 15 14 13 12

For more information about Albert Whitman & Company,
visit our web site at www.albertwhitman.com

Contents

1 · Spotlight Magicians

CINDY TEMPLE dashed around the corner with her arms full of books. She laughed when she saw the red motorbike, parked in its usual place behind the bookmobile. The motorbike belonged to the librarian, Terri Firestone.

"When I'm a librarian, I'm going to have a motorbike, too," thought Cindy. "A red one."

Cindy glanced at the roof of the bookmobile. She saw the red-haired young man who had been coming to make signs for the bookmobile. He was putting up one now. It was about the magic show, the last special show of the summer for the neighborhood kids who came to the bookmobile.

"You're late, P. Nelson Edward!" Cindy called. "You told Jay and Dexter and me that you'd turn into a pumpkin if you ever stayed late. You don't look like a pumpkin to me."

P. Nelson pushed his curly red hair off his forehead. "I didn't know it was so late. I've got to go. But first I've got to finish this sign. It's my masterpiece."

Just then a tall thin man with a silver beard and a heavy silver-headed cane crossed the street to the bookmobile. Cindy had seen him before, walking up and down. Now he glanced at P. Nelson Edward. "Not a bad job on a sunny day, eh?" he asked, stroking his beard.

P. Nelson looked down. "Oh, making signs? No, sir, not bad at all."

The man swung his silver cane slowly. He glanced at a big silver watch on his wrist. Then he looked up at P. Nelson once more. The silver rims on his dark glasses glinted in the sun. "How do you get up there?" he asked.

"It's easy," said P. Nelson. "There's the bumper, a window ledge, and a couple of hand grips. That's all there is to it."

The man nodded. Then he glanced over at Terri's red motorbike. He walked over to it and bent down to examine it closely. Then he turned and walked on, still swinging his silver cane.

"Who's he?" asked Cindy.

P. Nelson shrugged. "I don't know. I've never spoken to him before." He turned to his sign. "I've got to finish this and get going."

Cindy smiled at him and walked up the steps of the bookmobile. Terri Firestone was putting away the books that had been returned. "What, more books?" she laughed when she saw Cindy. "I've never known such a fast reader."

Cindy leaned against the counter with her armful of books. "I have," she said. "My mother. Most of these are hers."

There was a thumping on top of the bookmobile. "That P. Nelson Edward!" Terri exclaimed. "He made today's sign. He had today's coffee and doughnut. He left. Then back he came an hour ago, all hot and flustered. I thought he was coming to see me. But no, he had a new design he wanted to add to that sign." She sighed.

"Maybe he's getting up enough nerve to ask

you for a date," said Cindy. "Do you suppose?"

"I can dream," smiled Terri. "Anyway, I'm glad he's made signs for our special programs. They let people know what's going on and get them to come to the bookmobile. But you kids are my best customers. You and P. Nelson. And Miss Beautiful."

Cindy laughed. "You mean Olga Ratchett. Jay and Dexter call her Cleopatra. I think she looks like someone in a spy movie."

Terri nodded. "She's here every afternoon, hunting for books. Tells me what a great librarian her aunt is—I guess she lives with her. Anyway, I won't see her today. I have a special appointment with the dentist. I lost a filling from a tooth last night."

"Where's your assistant?" asked Cindy. "Will she keep the bookmobile open?"

"Bonnie's home with a cold. The library downtown is sending a substitute. She should be here now. Maybe there's a mix-up. Anyway, I only need someone for the next two days. Then the bookmobile goes into the garage for an overhaul."

"I'll miss it," Cindy said. "This is a good place for a bookmobile."

"It should be, the university's so close," said Terri. "And Ye Olde Shopping Center's right across the street. I love those quaint shops. And there's a shoe repair, a laundry, a drugstore—everything." She spread her arms wide. "And now: a library!"

"And a magic show," added Cindy. "I hope everybody comes to it."

"I know how hard you and Jay and Dexter have been working on it," said Terri. "I'm sure we'll have a good crowd. And if they come to the magic show, they'll be reminded of the bookmobile. They can start thinking about its grand reopening, painted and filled with new books."

"We've got some great acts ready," said Cindy, "but I wish I knew a magic trick to keep books from sliding—" And she stooped to pick up a book from the floor.

"That reminds me," Terri said. "Look in the closet behind the counter. There's a surprise for you, a kind of thank-you for helping with the magic show."

"Something for me?" Cindy asked, peering into the little closet. "It's a book bag! All in patchwork like your shirt. Did you make it?"

Terri nodded. "I make everything. Just from scraps. People can't tell whether my shirt is an old curtain or my curtain is an old shirt."

Cindy held up the book bag. "So many pockets! I can put everything I need in here." She reached into her sweater pocket. "I'll start with my notebook. I always carry a notebook in case there's a mystery. And there usually is."

"A mystery?" asked Terri.

"Didn't I tell you? Jay and Dexter and I have a sort of detective club. We call it the Spotlight Club. We've solved lots of mysteries, real ones."

"Well, I have one for you," said Terri. "Why doesn't P. Nelson ask me for a date?"

Cindy laughed. She had no answer. She picked up a book from the counter. It was with the books to be put away. "Here's a book about magic. May I take it out today? I'll bring it back tomorrow when all the books have to be turned in."

"Sure," Terri said. "I think P. Nelson just brought it back. Here, I'll write your name down and stamp the card."

Cindy was tucking the book into her new book bag when there was a loud knocking overhead. The skylight opened, and P. Nelson Edward looked down.

"Knock, knock, may I come in? I'm about ready to go. Anything else I can do?"

Terri and Cindy tilted their heads to look up. His curly red hair fell over his face as he leaned down.

"Hey, while you're up there, how about fixing the catch on the skylight window?" asked Terri. "That's one more thing out of order around here."

P. Nelson looked at the catch. "It's missing a part," he announced.

"Okay," said Terri. "I'll add it to my list of things to be fixed."

"I have to be going," P. Nelson said, still looking down into the bookmobile.

"Wait, I have an idea," said Terri suddenly. "Cindy and Jay and Dexter are coming to my place for chili tonight. We're going to work on the magic show. Maybe you'd like to join us."

"I accept," said P. Nelson. "I love chili and I love magic. I'll bring the fixings for a super salad. I'm no chef, though. I'm a chemist. Or at least I'm studying to be one, working my way through graduate school. And now I've lost my great job. I'll have to find another one in a hurry. Maybe as a sign painter. I've had lots of experience here."

"I'm sorry you lost your job," said Terri.

"It was an important project for an important person," said P. Nelson grandly. "But today is the last day. Ah, well, it isn't the end of the world. If I'm coming to your house for supper, I need your address."

"I thought you'd never ask," said Terri. She wrote her address and telephone number and handed them up to him. "Around six for supper."

P. Nelson put the address in his pocket. "I'll be there with the salad," he called down. Then he pulled his head back from the skylight window and shut it.

Terri walked over to the closet and looked at herself in a mirror on the back of the door. "Why can't I be like Olga Ratchett?" she asked. "Beautiful."

"Does P. Nelson think Olga's beautiful?" asked Cindy.

"He doesn't know her," Terri said, turning around. "He's never even met her. So that's lucky. For me, anyway."

14

"What about that job of his?" asked Cindy.

Terri shook her head. "I don't know much about it. Something about helping somebody work on some important project. I don't know who, and I don't know what. Just part-time. Imagine not having to be at work until 10:30! That isn't a job, it's a vacation, no matter how important it is." She peered at herself again. "Maybe if I didn't wear my glasses I'd look better. I only wear them to look older and dignified."

She pulled her glasses off and tried to open the drawer under the counter. It stuck. "One more thing to fix," she said as the drawer came open and she put her glasses away. Then she looked at her watch. "My new helper hasn't come. And I've got to get to the dentist. I'll just have to close early."

Watching Terri hunt for a card to make a notice, Cindy asked, "Who is your new assistant?"

"I've forgotten her name. It's something long. She's retired and just works part-time. I haven't met her," Terri said while she wrote EMERGENCY CLOSING on the card.

She lifted her red helmet down from the closet shelf. "I'll put the sign on the door. Oh, look at all those books to put away! And all the rest coming in tomorrow."

"Jay and I can come early tomorrow morning and help," said Cindy. "At eight-thirty."

Terri nodded. "Great. Now, what about tonight? I know—after the dentist, I have to pick up my shoes at Ye Olde Bootery. Why don't you and Jay and Dexter meet me there at five-thirty? I'll lead you to my place."

Outside, P. Nelson was just packing up his paints and brushes. "See you at six, P. Nelson," Terri said, fastening her helmet.

"At six," he answered. "One salad, one P. Nelson."

Terri gave Cindy a wink, kicked the starter on her motorbike, and was off. Cindy and P. Nelson watched the red motorbike chug up the street.

"What a racket!" P. Nelson exclaimed. "You can hear her a mile away. How can she stand that noise?"

"Noise doesn't seem to bother her," said Cindy. She looked at the sign on top of the bookmobile and said, "You're such a good sign painter. Maybe tonight you'll help me make the big cards we need for one magic trick. The man at Ye Happy Laundry said he'd give me some of the cardboard pieces he uses to package the shirts."

"Sure, I'll help," said P. Nelson.

Cindy started across the street to Ye Happy Laundry. A bright green sports car wheeled around the corner. "Too fast," thought Cindy, glancing at the driver, a fat man with a bald head. "Probably his hair blew off because he was going too fast."

On her way back with the cardboard, she saw Olga Ratchett walking with her dog toward the bookmobile. "They're both too beautiful," she decided. Then she stopped in her tracks.

Olga Ratchett's beautiful face was bright with anger. She did not see Cindy. She was staring at P. Nelson. And the next moment Olga Ratchett hissed through her teeth, "You fool! Don't you know what time it is?"

P. Nelson started to say something, then he stopped. He turned on his heel and walked away. He did not look back.

Cindy stared after him. What was that about? P. Nelson had told Terri he didn't even know Olga Ratchett!

2 · Angry About What?

CINDY STARED at Olga Ratchett and her big black Afghan hound. The two were a lot alike, Cindy decided.

Olga was dressed in a black turtleneck shirt and black pants. Long gold earrings swung from her ears. Around her neck was a gold chain with a pendant. The pendant was shaped like an eye, its center a large red jewel. On one finger she wore a gold ring shaped like a serpent with its tail in its mouth. The snake's ruby eye flashed in the sun. Like Olga Ratchett's anger, thought Cindy.

The dog's collar was gold colored, studded with red jewels. The leash was a long gold chain.

Both Olga and her dog were thin and graceful. People always turned to look at them.

Suddenly the big Afghan gave a small, short bark. He tugged at his leash and tried to reach Cindy. His big feathery tail wagged back and forth.

Cindy bent down to pat the dog's silky back. Olga Ratchett yanked at the gold leash and started up the steps of the bookmobile. She stared at the door.

"Closed!" she said, frowning. "It can't be!"

Cindy glanced up. "Well, it's closed now, but it will be open in the morning."

"In the morning!" exclaimed Olga Ratchett. "What about today? Today is when I want to take books out! Not tomorrow! Today! Right now! Where is that librarian? Can't she be called? What right has she to close like this?"

Cindy swallowed. "She had to go to the dentist. Her assistant didn't come. But the library will be open by nine tomorrow."

"Not until nine tomorrow!" said Olga angrily. "That doesn't suit me at all. I need the book now."

"I'm sorry," Cindy said. "My brother Jay and I are coming here to meet the librarian early, at eight-thirty. I'm sure she'd let you in then. We would come earlier, but we always have breakfast with Mom before she leaves for work."

Olga Ratchett pulled at the dog's leash. She said, "All the books have to be returned tomorrow. I want to take one out now. There's no excuse for this!"

Suddenly Cindy heard Jay's voice calling, "Cindy!" He stopped his bike in front of her. She bowed, "Cindy Temple at your service," she said.

"We've got to meet Dex at his house now to get the things from his attic. The things for the magic show," said Jay.

Olga glanced at Cindy and Jay. She swung the eye-shaped pendant angrily. Then she turned and started off.

"Wow!" Jay whispered. "What's Cleopatra so mad about?"

"I think we have a mystery," whispered Cindy. "P. Nelson said he didn't know Olga Ratchett. But he does. And she was really mad at him about something. Something about the time. And now she's upset because the bookmobile is closed early. And"

All at once Cindy stopped. "There's that strange man with the silver cane. Look!"

The Spotlight detectives watched as the man walked toward Olga Ratchett and her dog. His dark glasses with the silver rims flashed in the sun. He took her arm and began talking. He seemed very angry.

Olga Ratchett jerked the leash on her dog and pulled away from the man with the silver cane. He shook it at her angrily. She walked away from him, her head held high.

The man did not move. He stared after her. He gripped his silver cane tightly. He did not take his eyes off Olga Ratchett.

While Cindy and Jay watched, the man turned slowly around. He faced the bookmobile. Cindy and Jay stared. He paid no attention to them. He reached into his pocket, still peering up at the bookmobile. Then he wrote something on a piece of paper, using a silver pen. After another look he folded the paper, put it in his pocket, and walked away, swinging his heavy cane.

Cindy and Jay stared after him and then at each other.

"Why was he so mad at Olga? What did he write down?" wondered Jay. "Let's go to Dexter's.

We've got to tell him everything."

"And I've got to write everything down," said Cindy, patting her notebook in her new book bag. "Let's hurry."

At Dexter's house the three Spotlighters did not talk about the magic show. They talked about their new mystery.

"This is our mystery so far," said Cindy. And she read:

1. P. Nelson Edward. He said he doesn't know Olga Ratchett. But he does. And she is very mad at him. Why? It had something to do with the time. Was he late? For what?

2. Olga Ratchett. Why was she angry with P. Nelson? Why was she so upset about the bookmobile being closed early?

3. The man with the silver cane. Why was he angry at Olga Ratchett? What did he write down? Was it something about the bookmobile? Or the sign?

"Maybe he just wants to be sure to remember when the magic show starts," said Dexter, pushing his glasses up on his forehead.

"Do you realize the show is day after tomorrow, and we're not nearly ready?" Cindy asked. She looked at her watch. "And do you realize it's time to meet Terri now?"

The three sped on their bikes to Ye Olde Bootery. Terri was just coming out with her shoes.

"We've got a lot to tell you!" said Cindy. "Remember, I said we solved mysteries? Well, we've got a new one."

"Let's talk about it over chili," suggested Terri. "We've got to beat P. Nelson to the apartment. Otherwise he may just go away. And we can't have that." She hopped on her motorbike and stepped on the starter. "I'll go slow so you can keep up with me."

The three detectives followed Terri. She stopped in front of a white house.

"It's pretty," said Cindy.

"Yes, it is, isn't it?" agreed Terri. "But I don't live here. I live over the garage. These nice people rent it to me."

After parking their bikes in the driveway, the three followed Terri up the garage stairs.

"It may not be elegant, but it's where I hang my elegant hat," she said, hanging her red helmet on a hook outside the door. A raincoat and other patchwork jackets hung on other hooks.

Terri unlocked the door. Soon lamps spread a cozy glow around the room.

"It's all patchwork!" exclaimed Cindy. "Just like my book bag."

"Just don't peek under anything—under every patchwork cover is a bushel basket or a box," laughed Terri. Then she showed them around. A patchwork screen hid the tiny kitchen. Pots, pans and plates were on a patchwork-covered crate. A big pot of chili was bubbling on the one burner.

"Now, all we need is P. Nelson Edward. And his salad," said Terri.

The telephone rang.

"I'm so popular," said Terri. "It must be my personality." She ran into the bedroom to answer the telephone. Soon she came back, frowning. "It was P. Nelson. He's not coming. He said something important had happened. He sounded upset."

"Upset?" asked Jay.

"He didn't sound like himself at all. He just said he couldn't come, and he said he had to go to Chicago tomorrow." Terri shook her head. "He was really upset. I could tell."

"In your bones?" asked Dexter, grinning.

"That's where Cindy always can tell things—in her bones."

Terri laughed. "Well, we've got to eat our chili, troops. And then to work, P. Nelson or no."

The three detectives and Terri clustered about a round table in the living room. "We're sitting on bushel baskets," warned Terri.

As they ate, they told Terri about the man with the silver cane. "He was really mad at Olga Ratchett about something," said Cindy. "And she was mad at P. Nelson."

Terri frowned and leaned forward. "If there's a mystery, Olga Ratchett is the guilty one. But guilty of what?"

Cindy and the boys looked at each other. Terri seemed to have no doubts about Olga. They weren't so sure.

"We've got to plan the rest of the magic show," said Terri, passing the chili around again.

"We have some good tricks," Jay said.

"We'll show you a few now," offered Dexter. "Unless you don't feel like it."

Terri had put her hand up to her head. "I want to help, but I have a terrible headache. I guess it's being without my glasses. I do need them. Why did I leave them in the bookmobile?"

"We'll go back for them," Jay said.

"Let's all go," suggested Terri. "I need the exercise."

"Exercise?" scoffed Dexter. "On a motorbike!"

"I've got a regular bike, too. This time I'll pedal like the rest of the people. Let's go, gang."

The four of them ran down the garage stairs to their bikes.

"Do you have lights on your bikes?" asked Terri.

"Headlights and reflectors on our bikes, and armband lights, too," said Jay.

"Then we're off," said Terri. "The Firefly Brigade." And they headed toward the bookmobile.

"I won't fool myself again about not needing my glasses," said Terri. "I need them, and that's that."

Jay was in the lead. He was the first one to see the flickering light in the bookmobile.

3 · Bookmobile Break-in

"DOUSE YOUR LIGHTS!" hissed Jay.

They quickly obeyed, then stared at the eerie light flickering on and off in the bookmobile.

"Someone's in there," whispered Cindy. "Or else it's bewitched."

"I'm going to find out who it is," answered Terri. She hopped off her bike and put down the kickstand.

"Wait!" said Dexter hoarsely.

"Wait for what?" Terri asked in a low voice. "Someone's in my bookmobile, and I want to find out what's going on." Suddenly she grabbed Jay's arm. "Look," she whispered urgently.

The skylight window was pushed up. A dark figure drew itself up out of the bookmobile and stood for a moment. Then the mysterious visitor climbed down and ran away. It happened so quickly there was no chance to race after the figure, already lost in shadows.

"Let's look inside," whispered Jay. "Maybe we can tell what they were up to."

Cindy, Dexter, and Terri kept close behind Jay. There was no sound. Terri reached into her jacket pocket and took out her key. "I wonder if anything was stolen," she said softly.

In a moment she was turning the key in the lock. With hearts pounding, the Spotlighters blinked as Terri switched on the light.

They stared around them.

"I know how your visitor climbed out—by stepping on the shelves," Dexter said, squinting through his glasses. Books were tumbled on the floor.

"I see," agreed Terri. "But why would anyone break in?" She walked over to the counter. "Even if someone was dying to read a book, the least he could do is wait until we opened in the morning."

Suddenly Jay whistled. "Take a look at this."

Cindy and Dexter hurried over and crouched next to Jay.

"A matchbook," breathed Cindy. Its silver lettering had caught her eye. "That's what the flickering light was. Matches. The visitor must have forgotten to bring a flashlight, and didn't want to turn the lights on to attract attention."

"But why?" asked Jay, scratching his head and looking around. "What was going on here? Nothing seems to have been taken."

"I'm not a detective like the rest of you," said Terri. "But since there are only books here, I can figure out that whoever it was must have wanted a book."

"But which one? And why?" asked Cindy. She leaned over and took the matchbook from Jay's hand. She read out loud: "Veronica and Parry, August 10."

"That's our only clue," said Dexter. "But what does it mean?"

"Mom has some matches from a golden wedding anniversary party," said Cindy. "They're like party favors. But this is silver printing, not gold. So maybe it's a silver wedding anniversary. Or even a wedding."

"Or maybe an announcement of twins," suggested Dexter. "Anyway, the matches give us a date."

Jay nodded. "It's something to go on. If we can find what it's all about, maybe we can find out who was here."

"Needle in a haystack," sighed Dexter.

"But we've done that before," Cindy reminded him. She put the matchbook in her new book bag. "We can look in the newspapers for some announcement, a silver anniversary or maybe a wedding or twins or an engagement party. Something. August 10 isn't very long ago."

"After all this excitement, I almost forgot why we came," said Terri. "My glasses. If someone stole them, I hope they get a headache."

She pulled open the drawer under the counter. "Here they are. And here's the new blotter. As long as we're here, let's put it in so the counter will be all clean and fresh for morning."

She pulled the old blotter out and threw it away. Dexter put the new one in. "Pink for a new day," he grinned.

"Well, I hope the new day gives us more clues," said Cindy. "So far we have only one—the matchbook." She glanced around the bookmobile. "I wonder who was here. And why? What could anyone want?"

"We'll have to figure everything out in the morning," said Terri. "I promised your folks you'd be home early, and here it is late." She started to open the door.

Cindy spoke up. "Maybe whoever it was hid and watched us. Maybe someone's waiting out there for us now."

Terri hesitated.

"Well, there are four of us and only one of them," said Dexter. "Cindy, you and Terri wait inside. Jay and I will go first and check."

The boys stepped cautiously out of the bookmobile and walked down the stairs. They stood in the dark and listened a moment. Jay walked quietly around the bookmobile while Dexter stood guard. There was no sound. And no sign of the intruder.

"The coast is clear," Jay announced, turning on his flashlight.

Cindy and Terri joined the boys. They all stood at the bottom of the bookmobile steps.

"You'd better go your way. I'll go mine," said

Terri. "We'll meet here at eight-thirty tomorrow morning, okay?"

"Not me," said Dexter. "I have to do Maxwell's lawn first. But I'll be here as soon as I can."

Terri turned on her bicycle light. In a moment she had cycled out of sight. They watched until they could no longer see the light. Then the three detectives walked over to their bikes. Cindy glanced over her shoulder. Could someone be watching them from the shadows? Listening to them?

"Let's get out of here," she whispered. "We can talk when we get home."

Jay nodded. They rode back to the Temple house quickly, single file, and put their bikes in the garage. "First, let's check the newspapers for some clue about this matchbook," said Jay. "Mom always keeps old newspapers till they make a big enough load for the paper drives in the neighborhood."

They walked into the house. Lights were burning brightly in the living room where Mrs. Temple sat reading. "How was your supper with Terri Firestone?" she asked.

Cindy laughed. "I'd forgotten all about that. So much has happened since!"

Mrs. Temple put her book down and shook her head. "Another mystery? I'll bet you three could find a mystery in a piece of toast."

"This one is a real one," insisted Cindy. "We were working on our magic show at Terri's apartment. Terri had left her glasses at the bookmobile, so we all rode our bikes over to get them."

"And guess what? Someone was inside with matches!" added Jay.

"Someone had sneaked in through the skylight," said Dexter.

"Yes, the skylight latch was broken," said Cindy. "That's how he got in. And then he got away before we could see who it was."

Mrs. Temple laughed. "Whoa, sleuths, I can hardly catch my breath."

"We have to find out who Veronica and Parry are," said Cindy, showing her mother the matchbook. "They may be celebrating a silver wedding anniversary. Maybe they're twins, just born. Or a couple just getting engaged or married. We have to look in the newspapers."

Mrs. Temple laughed. "Last week's papers and this week's papers are in the box in the hall." She picked up her book and peered across the top at the vanishing Spotlighters. "Good luck," she called.

Cindy picked out papers for August 10, 11, and 12. She looked for birth announcements. Jay looked for wedding anniversaries. Dexter looked for engagements and weddings. The only sound in the hallway was the hurried rustling of newspapers.

Suddenly Dexter yelped. "Here it is!"

Cindy and Jay looked over his shoulder. Sure enough! There was an article about a wedding of Veronica someone and Parry someone on August 10. And there was a photograph of the reception. The three detectives examined it closely.

"Nobody we know," said Dexter.

"Look at this man, with his back to the camera," said Cindy. "That could be the man with the cane."

"It could be anybody," said Jay.

"This lady in the big hat. It could be Olga Ratchett," said Cindy.

"It could and it couldn't," said Dexter. "We have to find out who was at the wedding."

Hastily the three detectives scanned the article. "Daughter of a chemistry professor at the university," murmured Cindy. "Over three hundred guests present."

"Three hundred guests!" groaned Jay. "Now we'll never be able to find out who dropped the matchbook."

"We can try," said Cindy. She peered once again at the photograph. Then she tore the page out and put it in her book bag. "Maybe it's someone we haven't met yet."

"At least we know what the silver matchbook meant," said Jay. "It was a wedding. And a wedding

reception. And one of the guests had a matchbook. And dropped it in the bookmobile tonight."

"Three hundred guests," said Dexter gloomily.

"Wait a minute," said Jay. "Three hundred guests. That's a lot. But the bride was a daughter of a chemistry professor at the university. So lots of the guests would probably be other university people. Other professors."

"Or students," said Cindy suddenly. "And P. Nelson is a chemistry student. Let's ask him if he's been to any good weddings lately."

Cindy reached into her book bag and withdrew the matchbook. She turned it over in her hand. "Silver, silver," she said out loud. Suddenly she snapped her fingers. "I know what that makes me think of. The man with the silver cane! The silver cane, the silver beard! Remember this afternoon when he wrote something down? With a silver pen?"

Jay nodded slowly. "He looked at the bookmobile. Or at the sign. And copied something down."

"Maybe he sketched the bookmobile and the skylight," said Cindy. "So he could climb in at night."

Jay nodded soberly. "That's just what he was doing. It must be."

The three detectives sat in silence for a moment. "Let's sleep on it," suggested Dexter.

"Meet you at the bookmobile when you're through mowing lawns, Dex," said Jay.

Later, in her room, Cindy looked at the newest items in her notebook before going to bed.

Query: What did the man with the cane draw?
Answer: A sketch of the bookmobile.
Query: Why did he draw that sketch?
Answer: So he could figure out the best way to break in.
Query: Where did the man get the matches?
Answer: From a wedding reception. But there were three hundred guests at the wedding.
Query: Who is the man with the cane?
Answer: I wish I knew.

Cindy closed her notebook and turned off her light. She dreamed of flickering lights in the dark and a man with a silver cane.

4 · Stolen Address

CINDY REACHED for her notebook as soon as her eyes were open the next morning. She read over what she had written the night before. Then she hurried to dress and ran downstairs.

Jay was already in the kitchen. He was slicing bananas onto three bowls of cereal.

"Mom's out in the backyard talking to the tomatoes," he grinned.

Cindy nodded and poured herself a glass of orange juice. "We've got to get over to the bookmobile to meet Terri. There has to be some other clue. Some footprints in the grass. Something. Something that we didn't notice last night."

Jay nodded. "We have to prove it was the man with the silver cane. Not just guess. Remember Mr.

Hooley's rule: we can't just guess. We have to prove everything we suspect."

Cindy opened her notebook. "You're right. And we *are* taking some things for granted. For instance, are we sure it was a man who broke in? Maybe it was Olga Ratchett! She really wanted a book, remember! I told you how angry she was when the bookmobile was closed yesterday."

"Who wants a library book enough to climb in through a skylight?" asked Jay, putting the three bowls on the kitchen table. "Not me, anyway."

"We've got to remember the Usher Rule, too," said Cindy thoughtfully. "We have to suspect the people we like as well as the bad guys. So just because we like P. Nelson Edward, that doesn't mean he couldn't have done something wrong. And remember, he's a chemistry student. So maybe he was at the reception. And maybe he broke into the bookmobile last night."

Cindy thought for a moment. "Besides, P. Nelson knew the skylight catch was broken. And he knew how to climb up. He told the man with the silver cane." She suddenly stopped and swallowed. "P. Nelson told the man with the silver cane how to climb up. It always comes back to the man with the silver cane."

Mrs. Temple came in from the backyard, holding a small tomato. "Look. It may not be big, but it's beautiful. And it's all ours." She set it on the middle of the table.

While they had breakfast, Jay and Cindy told her more about the mystery. "I think you must have secret mystery magnets sewn into the soles of your shoes. Mysteries are always following you around. They never follow me. For instance, this morning I saw someone walking a big dog in the alley behind our yard. Now, if I had been a detective, I'd have wondered what that girl was doing in the alley. Spying on our tomatoes?"

Jay and Cindy laughed. As soon as they had stacked the breakfast dishes, they started out of the kitchen.

"Remember, loves, this is my night to work late," Mrs. Temple reminded them. "You're having supper with the Tates."

"We remember. We remember *everything*," grinned Jay. "And we remember everything because Cindy writes everything down in that notebook."

Cindy clapped her hand to her forehead. "And I forgot my notebook!" she exclaimed, running back into the kitchen. "And my book bag. Plus all the magic stuff."

Mrs. Temple walked out onto the front porch with them. "Aren't you taking back those library books? I see they're all on the hall table."

"This afternoon, Mom," said Jay.

When Terri Firestone rode up to the bookmobile on her red motorbike, Cindy and Jay had just arrived.

"What perfect timing," laughed Terri, taking off her helmet. "I've got to admit I'm glad you're here to open up. Even in broad daylight, I don't want to go in alone. Not after last night. Isn't that silly? Of course my new helper should be coming soon."

Jay glanced down. "We thought we'd look around the bookmobile for footprints or something," he said. "But it's all cement."

"I'll open up," said Terri, reaching into the pocket of her patchwork jacket. She made a face. "I must have left the bookmobile key in my other jacket."

"I'll try to get in through the skylight window," offered Jay.

Terri shook her head. "You won't have to. I always have a key hidden in a secret place. I've had to use it twice this week. I wonder what that proves about my being absentminded?"

She walked around to the other side of the bookmobile. Cindy and Jay followed her. Just then Cindy looked over her shoulder and saw the man with the silver cane. He was walking quickly by. Cindy stared. Was he waiting for a chance to get into the bookmobile? Was he watching Terri?

Terri was kneeling down and reaching under the bookmobile, just behind the front tire.

In a moment she stood up, holding a key. "If you do that a few times, you'll remember for sure that it's hard cement instead of soft grass under this bus!"

"Where was the key?" asked Jay curiously.

"I have a magnetic thingamajig under there," Terri answered. "I have to remember to put the key back in the holder each time I use it. Otherwise sometime I'll lock myself out for sure."

"The man with the silver cane just walked by,"

whispered Cindy to Jay. "But he's gone now."

Jay raised his eyebrows.

Terri opened the door of the bookmobile and handed the key to Jay. He replaced it in the magnetic holder under the bookmobile.

"I can't believe the visitor didn't leave one single clue. Except the matchbook," said Cindy, as they followed Terri into the bookmobile. Suddenly Cindy gasped and picked up a silver pen from the desk. "This wasn't here last night, was it?"

Terri looked at the pen, frowning. "I've never seen it before."

"That's funny," said Jay, "because we looked all around the desk last night. On top, on the floor, everywhere. I know we'd have seen it."

"Silver pen," said Cindy. "The man with the silver cane had a silver pen, remember?" She turned the pen in her hand. "Look, initials. D.D." She handed the pen to Jay.

"D.D. I don't know who that could be," said Jay.

"The man with the cane. Who else? This proves he was here!" decided Cindy.

"Remember Mr. Hooley's Rule," Jay reminded

her. "We don't know for sure it was the man with the silver cane. We're still guessing. It could have been Olga Ratchett. Or P. Nelson Edward."

Terri Firestone broke into laughter. "P. Nelson Edward! You must be joking. Of course it wasn't P. Nelson."

"How do you know?" asked Jay. "We have a rule that says you have to suspect someone whether you like him or not. It's the Usher Rule."

Terri stopped laughing. "Well, for one thing, I know he didn't. And for another, he told me so."

"Told you? When?" asked Cindy.

"He called again last night after I got home. To say he was sorry about not coming. Then I told him about our little adventure. I told him everything. He was very interested. He said he couldn't imagine who would do a thing like that—breaking into the book-mobile." Terri looked at Jay and Cindy in turn. "So you see? He couldn't have done it. If he had, he'd have told me!"

Cindy groaned. "You can't believe everything someone tells you. Especially in a mystery."

Terri looked stubborn. "Well, I can promise you it wasn't P. Nelson. It could have been anyone else, but not P. Nelson. He's so—honest! And so nice! Why don't you suspect someone you haven't even met? Some stranger?"

Jay and Cindy exchanged glances. Cindy sighed. Then she looked thoughtfully at the desk. Suddenly she leaned over.

On the blotter, the fresh pink blotter Dexter had put there last night, was the impression of some writing. "Look," she pointed. "Someone wrote something here. Someone wrote on thin paper—the writing went right through. Whoever wrote was pressing too hard on the pencil or pen. Pen! Of course, that's it." She turned the blotter around and peered at it. And then she gasped.

There on the blotter was her name: Cindy Temple. And her address: 6910 Random Street.

Cindy stared. "My name! My address! But why?"

Jay leaned over and looked at the impression on the blotter carefully. "We put the blotter in just before we left last night," he said, frowning.

Cindy nodded. "Whoever we saw leaving must have come back later," she said. "But why? Just to write down things about me? What for?"

47

Terri glanced at the blotter as she opened the closet door. "I can't understand it," she said, putting her helmet on the shelf. "Why would she write your name down?"

Jay grinned. "*She*? You sure want Olga Ratchett to be the guilty one, don't you?"

Terri nodded. "Of course."

"But it could have been anyone," said Cindy. "The man with the silver cane, P. Nelson, anyone."

Terri laughed. "There you go again. P. Nelson! He wouldn't do anything!"

"But I have to write him down as a suspect," protested Cindy.

"You may as well write me down," said Terri. "That wouldn't be any sillier than P. Nelson."

"Except that you were with us the whole time," said Cindy. "He wasn't."

"Maybe I'm a witch and maybe I've bewitched this bookmobile," teased Terri. She looked behind Cindy toward the open door and said, "Good morning!"

A tall, angular woman stepped quickly up the steps and looked around at the Spotlighters and Terri.

"Good morning, one and all," she smiled. "I'm ready for work. But it's going to be more like fun. I've never worked in a bookmobile before. Just in a regular library. Or the one at the university."

Her gray-streaked hair was drawn into a tight bun at the back of her head. A pair of tinted glasses hung from a chain around her neck. A short pencil sat behind each ear.

"University," thought Cindy. She nudged Jay.

"You must be my helper for the next two days," said Terri, turning to the tall woman. "I was expecting you yesterday. I guess there was a mix-up. I can certainly use your help."

The tall woman laughed. "Good! I'm glad to be needed. And yes, there must have been a mix-up yesterday. They clearly stated today. Today and tomorrow."

Her long fingers reached for her glasses. She blinked twice and set the round tinted glasses on her nose.

Terri pointed. "There must be a million books that have to be returned today." She turned to Cindy and Jay. "That leaves you two free to work on the magic show."

"We'll need it," Jay admitted.

"These fine young detectives are Jay and Cindy Temple," explained Terri. "My friends and helpers."

The tall woman peered through her glasses at Jay and Cindy. "Temple, Temple," she said under her breath. She rubbed one of the pencils back and forth behind her ear. "Detectives? How unusual."

She crossed her arms. "Just call me Aunt Margaret. I have a last name, of course, but it's too long for anyone but me to remember. Sometimes I can hardly remember it myself!" She blinked once more and nodded her head sharply so that her glasses fell off her nose and landed on her chest with a little thud. "I'm everybody's aunt, more or less. I know everyone, and everyone knows me. That's an exaggeration of course. I like to exaggerate. But I *am* the neighborhood aunt, simple as that. If you don't have an aunt, you have one now."

Cindy reached into her book bag and pulled out the clipping about the wedding.

"If you worked at the university library, maybe you know some of these people," she said, handing the clipping to Aunt Margaret. Aunt Margaret replaced her glasses on her nose and peered at the clipping.

"Of course I know them! Lovely people! Beautiful bride! Wonderful wedding! That's my umbrella there at the edge. The photographer didn't manage to get me into the picture. But I was there, all the same."

What luck! thought Cindy. Then she asked, "Do you know this lady in the big hat?" Aunt Margaret laughed. "Know her! I should say I do. She's my niece. I'm her real aunt. I told her not to wear that silly hat, but she insisted. Olga always has things her own way."

5 · Scared!

OLGA! CINDY SWALLOWED. So Olga *had* been at the wedding, according to Aunt Margaret.

"Did anyone have a cane?" asked Cindy.

"Cane? Oh my yes. There were canes all over the place. Sometimes I think men like to carry canes the way women like to wear hats."

"So Olga Ratchett is your niece," said Terri. "She comes in here almost every day."

Aunt Margaret turned to Terri. "She does, does she? Well, that's news to me. She never was much of a reader. If having bookmobiles makes readers out of Olgas, then I'm all for them. Well, we'd better get to work. Enough gossip!"

Terri smiled. "I'll show you where the cards are that belong to all these books," she said, pointing to the piles of books on the counter. "And then we'll just put the books away."

Aunt Margaret set her glasses on her nose again and clapped her hands once. "Excellent. Let's get started."

"That leaves Jay and me in the clear to work on the magic show," said Cindy, putting the clipping away. "We'll just wait outside for Dexter."

Aunt Margaret raised her eyebrows. She took a pencil from behind her ear and licked the tip of it. "Could I ask you one great favor? I wouldn't normally ask detectives, but you seem to be regular children as well." She blinked twice and looked at Jay and Cindy.

"Sure," Jay grinned.

Aunt Margaret smiled. "Excellent. I've left a monstrosity of a dog tied up out there. He's terribly clever and might find a way to get loose. And Olga would never forgive me. She just went to Chicago for the day. She left me in charge."

"We'd be glad to check on him," said Cindy. "We'll make sure he's tied securely."

"Right," said Jay. "Olga Ratchett's dog is worth watching."

Aunt Margaret nodded briefly and clapped her hands again. "Excellent," she said under her breath.

"See you later, Terri," said Cindy. "We'll go on home after we meet Dex. We're going to finish working on the magic show. Don't worry about it."

"I'll worry," Terri assured her, "because the show is tomorrow. Hey, what about all the library books you were going to bring back?"

Jay answered. "This afternoon. We need a truck to carry them all."

"My, my," said Aunt Margaret. "You must read a lot."

Jay and Cindy walked out of the bookmobile. The big Afghan wagged a friendly tail.

"Olga Ratchett's aunt," exclaimed Jay.

"And Olga was at the wedding," said Cindy.

"So was Aunt Margaret," Jay reminded her.

They made sure the dog was fastened securely and then walked across the street. They sat on a park bench to wait for Dexter.

"Olga wanted that book so much yesterday. But she's gone off to Chicago without it," said Cindy.

"Maybe she got the book last night," said Jay. "We don't know."

"Or maybe she sent her Aunt Margaret in to get it this morning," Cindy said, getting out her notebook. She wrote for a moment and then she looked up at the bookmobile. Cindy shivered. "Maybe the man with the silver cane is waiting for me. Watching me right now."

"Don't worry," said Jay. "He wouldn't do anything right here in broad daylight. The stores are open. There are lots of people around. I'm not worrying."

"He didn't write down *your* name," retorted Cindy. "I'm so worried I can't even think about the magic show. He might be waiting for me at home this minute."

"We don't have to go home if you don't want to," Jay said. "We'll work on the show over at Dexter's today. Mrs. Tate and Anne said they found lots of costumes for us in the attic."

Cindy looked at her notebook. "It really could have been Olga we saw last night. She wears pants and a sweater." She shut her eyes. "I'm trying to remember something."

"How can you remember something if you don't know what it is you're trying to remember?" asked

Jay. "That's a neat trick if you can do it."

"Sssssh," said Cindy. "I'm concentrating. It has something to do with Olga Ratchett."

Suddenly her eyes opened.

"This morning! Mom said there was a girl with a big dog in our alley. It was Olga Ratchett. It had to be! And maybe she was waiting for me—waiting to get me!"

"Maybe you're right," Jay said thoughtfully. "But she didn't."

"Yet," said Cindy.

"There's Dex," said Jay suddenly. He whistled their secret Spotlight whistle. Dexter looked around. He ran across the street to Jay and Cindy.

"Wait till you hear," Jay started to say.

Dexter interrupted. "I've got news—big news! I found out who the man with the silver cane is!"

"Who?" asked Cindy.

Dexter kept talking. "I saw him. I followed him. I followed him all the way to his house, 666 Frew Street. I saw him open the door with a key, so I knew he must live there. But I didn't know how I could find out his name. It wasn't on the mailbox."

"Well, how did you? What is it?" asked Jay.

"Let me explain the way it happened. I had to find out his name. I remembered I'd passed a stationery store on the way. I went there and got a clipboard. And paper. And a pencil. You're right, Cindy, about always carrying supplies like that with you. You never know when you need them."

"Hurry up," said Jay impatiently.

"Well, I got everything, and then I went up and rang his doorbell. But he didn't answer."

Cindy groaned.

"A lady did. I said I was getting people to sign my petition."

"Your petition? What petition?" asked Jay.

"Of course I didn't have one. I made it up," answered Dexter proudly. "I said I was trying to get signatures. About noise pollution. Signatures of everyone in the neighborhood who was against noise. You know, trying to keep the neighborhood quiet."

"Keep talking," said Jay.

"She signed her name," continued Dexter. "Virginia Pipestone. And then she said, 'Wait a minute. I know the doctor will want to sign, too. He's home this morning.' She went in. In a minute she was out again, with his signature." Dexter looked at Jay and

Cindy. "His name is Dr. Drummond. She's his secretary."

Cindy started to write in her notebook. "What kind of doctor?" she asked.

"I don't know," Dexter said. "But wait. Here comes the funny part. I was just leaving, and she said, 'It's too bad Mr. Edward doesn't work here any more. He'd have been glad to sign it—if only you'd been here yesterday. He hates noise.' "

"Mr. Edward!" said Jay. "But—"

Dexter nodded. "I wanted to find out for sure. So I said, 'Not Mr. *Edward* Edward, by chance?' And she said, 'No. Mr. P. Nelson Edward!' "

Jay whistled. Cindy said, "I'm exhausted. P. Nelson Edward—working for the man with the silver cane!"

Dexter took his clipboard out from under his arm. He removed the paper and handed it to Jay and Cindy. They read the signatures. Virginia Pipestone. Dr. David Drummond.

"Dr. David Drummond!" whispered Cindy. "D.D.!"

6 · Hidden Message

DEXTER PUSHED his glasses up. "What are you talking about? What's D.D.?"

Quickly Jay and Cindy told Dexter about the pen with the initials D.D. And Cindy's name and address on the new blotter. And about meeting Aunt Margaret. Everybody's Aunt Margaret. Olga Ratchett's *real* Aunt Margaret.

"So it must have been Dr. David Drummond, the man with the silver cane, last night," said Dexter thoughtfully.

"Remember Mr. Hooley's Rule," Jay reminded him. "Just because we found his pen doesn't mean he was there. We've found out that P. Nelson worked for him. He could have taken the pen by mistake. And then left it at the bookmobile last night."

"P. Nelson lied about knowing Olga Ratchett. And he lied about knowing Dr. David Drummond, the man with the cane," said Cindy firmly. "He said he'd never spoken to him before. And he's been *working* for him. If you lie about one thing, you lie about other things."

She glanced over to the bookmobile. "Where are all our suspects? Dr. Drummond? Olga Ratchett? P. Nelson?"

Jay held up three fingers. "Well, Dr. Drummond just signed Dexter's paper, so we know he's at home. And Aunt Margaret says Olga is in Chicago for the day."

"But we're not sure Aunt Margaret is telling the truth," said Dexter. "Or maybe she thinks she's telling the truth. Maybe Olga fooled her. Maybe Olga didn't go anywhere."

"Maybe she's just waiting for me," whispered Cindy.

"Well, where's P. Nelson Edward?" asked Jay.

"In Chicago," said Dexter. "Remember, he told Terri."

Cindy looked at the boys with raised eyebrows. "That's what he *told* Terri. That he would be in Chicago today. That doesn't mean that's the truth, of course."

"Hmmm," said Dexter. "Olga and P. Nelson in Chicago. Together?"

"We don't know a thing," said Cindy gloomily.

"Yes, we do," said Jay. "We know Aunt Margaret is at the bookmobile helping Terri. And Terri is in the bookmobile," said Jay. "And the Spotlight Club is sitting here staring at the bookmobile."

Dexter pulled his glasses down on his nose. "Whoever wrote Cindy's name down must want to see her," he said.

Cindy swallowed. "Let's stay here," she said. She frowned. "It could be Dr. Drummond, the man with the cane. Or Olga Ratchett. Or P. Nelson Edward."

"Well, if it's P. Nelson, you have nothing to be afraid of," said Jay. "He wouldn't hurt a fly."

"Anyway, I'd feel safer if I had a disguise to wear," said Cindy. She reached into her book bag. "How about these red-tinted glasses? The ones I wear for that one magic trick."

She put the red-tinted glasses on and turned to look at Jay.

"What a nice sunburn you have," she said.

She turned to Dexter. "And what pretty red hair you're wearing today."

She looked around. "Pink sky, pink grass, pink people," she announced.

Suddenly she gasped and clutched Jay.

"What's wrong?" he asked, looking at her.

Cindy pointed across the street.

"The sign!" she said. "Look at the sign on the bookmobile."

The two boys looked. "It looks all right to me," said Dexter.

Cindy shook her head. She pulled off the red glasses and handed them to Jay. He put them on and looked across at the sign. "What does it mean?"

he asked slowly. "Dex, you read it."

Dexter grabbed the glasses from Jay and put them over his own. "Just call me six-eyes," he muttered. Then he whistled. "It says 7938 SM." He took the red glasses off and looked at the sign. Then he put them on again. "There's more! It says *LAST ONE*. Now you see it and now you don't," he added, sliding the red-tinted glasses up and down on his nose.

"It's a secret message!" said Jay. "Otherwise it wouldn't be hidden like that. But what does it mean?"

"Wait a minute," Cindy said. "Is a message really there? Could it be an accident and just happen to look like those numbers and letters?"

Dexter shook his head. "No way. We had an experiment like this in science. Here, Cindy, take the glasses, but don't put them on yet. See that fancy design? It has yellow and blue and green and red. Look at the B. See? Now look through the glasses. Keep looking at the B. The red part of the B is missing now, isn't it? Because you're looking through the red glasses. Now it looks like a 3, doesn't it?"

B

Cindy nodded. She slipped the glasses up and down on her nose. "P. Nelson made the sign," said Cindy slowly. "So he had to be the one who put the secret message there."

"And what does it mean?" asked Dexter. "If we knew that, maybe we'd know who was supposed to read it."

Cindy put the red glasses on once more and peered at the sign. She read the numbers and copied them in her notebook, 7938 SM. The three detectives stared at the brightly painted sign on the bookmobile.

"Wait a minute," said Jay slowly. "Remember when the man with the silver cane—Dr. Drummond —wrote something down? Remember? Well, he must have been copying down the message!"

The three detectives stared at each other.

"He was wearing dark glasses with silver rims," said Cindy. "They could have been red-tinted glasses!"

"But what does it mean?" frowned Dexter.

The three detectives sat and stared at the sign. They took turns putting on the red glasses. "7938 SM," said Cindy. "And then LAST ONE. Last what?"

"We'll never be able to figure it out," said Jay. "We could *ask* P. Nelson. But he might lie and we'd never find out what this mystery is about."

Cindy wrote in her notebook, "P. Nelson. Fooled everyone. Fooled us. Fooled Terri."

Suddenly Jay snapped his fingers. "I know! I bet the number is a telephone number in disguise! SMAllwood 7938!"

"You're a genius!" said Dexter, pushing his glasses down on his nose. "That's got to be it!"

He stood up. "Let's go home and call that number. We can find out something, anyway. Maybe we'll recognize the voice that answers. Let's go!"

"What about staying here to watch?" asked Cindy.

"We could ask Terri to keep an eye out for our suspects," suggested Dexter.

Cindy groaned. "We can't do that. She tells P. Nelson everything. Besides, Aunt Margaret is there. She could be a suspect. She could be a spy that Olga Ratchett planted there."

"I think it's more important to go home and make that phone call than to wait around here any more," said Jay. "Everyone can see us. Nobody will do anything anyway as long as we're here."

"Agreed," Dexter said.

Cindy nodded and put the red-tinted glasses back in her book bag. "If they could think up messages that can be read with red glasses, then they can think up other things. Maybe x-ray glasses. They're probably looking right into my brain!"

The three detectives hurried to Dexter's. No one suspicious in sight. "Anne's home," Dexter said. "If we have to go anywhere, we can talk her into taking us. Big sisters are handy sometimes."

They ran up the porch steps. Anne was in the kitchen. "I'm experimenting with a new kind of cake mix," she said. "You can be the first to try it."

"Good," said Dexter, as he walked to the phone.

"I'll dial, you talk," he said to Jay.

"And I'll take notes," said Cindy, getting out her notebook.

"What's the number again?" asked Dexter.

Cindy looked in her notebook. "Here it is," she said. "It's 7938 SM. But why are the numbers first?"

Jay said, "Just to fool us, I think."

Dexter dialed SMA-7938. He pressed the telephone to his ear and waited.

"What number are you calling?" asked the operator. Dexter told her. "I'm sorry, there is no such number in Kenoska."

Dexter frowned and hung the telephone up. "Well, it's not in Kenoska. Maybe Chicago."

They tried again. No luck.

"Maybe it isn't a telephone number after all," said Jay. "But what else could it be?"

The Spotlighters stared at the telephone. Finally Jay said, "I guess I was wrong. But it's got to mean something."

"Maybe it's an address. In code," said Cindy.

"A license plate!" said Dexter, jumping up. "That's what it is, a license plate number! They're different in every state. All we have to do is find out what state has plates like that. And then find out who owns a car with the plate. And then all we have to do—" His voice trailed off and he sat down dejectedly.

Jay said, "We're stumped. Cindy, why don't you write down some things we know? Then maybe we can figure out the message."

Cindy took notes while all three talked. Then she read:

P. Nelson was working for Dr. David Drummond.
But P. Nelson said he'd never spoken to him, didn't know who he was.
P. Nelson's sign had a hidden message.
Query: Was the message for Dr. Drummond?
Answer: Probably.
Query: What does the message mean anyway?

The boys shook their heads. Cindy leafed back through her notes. She looked at the bottom of a page. She frowned. "I'm getting messy in my old age. I've written the number all squinched in at the bottom. I'll just recopy it." She flipped to a new page and flipped back again to look at the number. Suddenly she stopped.

"Hey," she said, pointing to the number she had written at the bottom of the page. "Look at it!"

"We did," said Jay.

"No, look. The way I wrote it. I didn't have room so I couldn't write it on one line. Look, it's a library book number. You know, the catalog number on the spine of a library book. Every book has a code. The code is written on the spine. That way you can find what you're looking for. You know how hard it is to find a certain book on our bookshelves, for example. If we had it all worked out like a library it would be easy. Anyway, that's what the number is. The library code. The code for a certain book!"

"I don't get it," said Jay.

"Well, you don't want to be a librarian the way I do," said Cindy. "I remember things like that. For instance, the two letters are the first two letters of the author's last name. SM could be for Smith or Smathers or Smitley, or something. There was a dot we didn't pay any attention to after the 3. So it's

793.8 SM. And that makes a difference."

"If you're right," said Jay slowly, "then who-ever broke into the bookmobile last night was look-ing for a special book. A book that P. Nelson had told about in the secret message on the sign. The sign about the magic show."

"I never noticed that about library books," said Dexter. "I just go in and ask where books on science are."

"Lazy," said Cindy. "Here, I'll show you. I've got a library book in my book bag."

"You've got everything in your book bag," said Dexter.

"Even your brains," said Jay. "I hope you never lose your book bag."

Cindy pulled out the book about magic that she'd checked out yesterday. She hadn't had time to read it.

"See," she said, pointing to the numbers on the spine of the book. "Every library book has numbers." She looked, then looked again. And gasped. The book almost slipped from her fingers.

"This is it!" she whispered. "This is the book the sign's all about! The book they're trying to get."

7 · *All Kinds of Dummies*

JAY GRABBED THE BOOK from Cindy. Dexter looked over Jay's shoulder at the number on the spine of the book.

"You're right," breathed Jay. "The same numbers. The same letters. This is it. This is the book someone wants!"

"And I've got it," said Cindy. "And I'm scared."

"Don't be silly," said Jay. "Dexter and I are here with you. And if anyone wants the book they can just ask us for it. That's easy."

"Nothing's easy," said Cindy. She took the book from Jay's grasp. "What's important about this book anyway? *Magic Here, There, Everywhere*, by Smuckers." She opened the book and quickly leafed through it. Then she shook it. "There's nothing in it," she announced.

"Let me look," said Jay. He examined the book carefully. "There are some pencil marks on some of the pages. Look. You can hardly see them." They took turns looking at the strange marks.

"It's a code!" said Cindy.

"Or else it's just someone doodling," suggested Dexter.

"No one doodles in a library book," said Cindy indignantly.

"They don't?" asked Jay innocently.

"They shouldn't," retorted Cindy.

Cindy opened her notebook and turned a page. "Book," she wrote. "Title: *Magic Here, There, Everywhere.*"

Query: Why important?
1. P. Nelson made a sign.
2. The sign had a secret message.
3. The secret message was the library code of this book.
Query: Why?
1. For someone to see.
2. Someone saw.

3. Someone tried to find the book by breaking into bookmobile at night.
4. They didn't get it (we have it).

Query: Who?
1. Dr. David Drummond?
2. Olga Ratchett?
3. P. Nelson Edward?
4. Aunt Margaret?
5. Or someone we haven't met?

"Well, nobody knows we have it," said Jay.

Suddenly Cindy stopped writing in her notebook. She stared at her notes. "I've got it. Don't you see? Whoever broke in couldn't find the book. So they looked in the files to see who had taken it out. It was me! That's why they wrote down my name and address."

Dexter pushed his glasses down on his nose. "Somebody wants the book. And now somebody knows you have it."

Cindy shivered. "Jay, go over to the window. See if anyone is waiting outside our house. Someone with a silver cane."

Jay peered next door. "No one. Just a squirrel."

"Maybe it's someone in disguise," said Cindy. "Someone small."

The boys grinned and Dexter said, "You're safe. You've got us to protect you."

"Let's be sensible," said Jay. "Someone saw this code number on the sign. The code number of this book. Someone was trying to find it last night. They couldn't find it, but they found out who had it. You."

He leaned forward earnestly. "They want the book, sure. But they don't want anyone to *know* they want it. Otherwise they'd have just asked for it, the way other people do."

Dexter nodded. "Right. So maybe they'll just watch and wait until it's been returned."

Cindy interrupted. "All the books are to be returned today. So they'll think I'm bringing it back. They don't know that we've seen the secret message. They don't know we've figured it out, either."

Anne called from the kitchen. "I thought you wanted me to be an audience for your magic tricks. Hurry up, if you want me. I have to go out."

Anne sat on the living room couch, drinking a glass of milk and eating a pretzel. Dexter strung up a sheet across the room. He sat in front of it, tapping a bongo drum softly.

Jay appeared from behind the sheet. A turban was wrapped around his head. He carried a blue box with a glass lid. "Please examine this box," he said, handing it to Anne.

Dexter thumped softly on the bongo drums.

Anne took the box, looked at it, shook it, and turned it over and over. "Well, it's blue. It doesn't open. And it's empty," she said finally.

"You're quite sure, Madam?" asked Jay.

"You may call me Ms.," said Anne.

At that moment Cindy appeared from behind the sheet. She wore long flowing scarves. Scarves dripped and drooped and drifted from her arms. A long scarf tied her hair back.

"Do not take your eyes from the blue box," Jay instructed Anne.

"Don't worry, I won't," she assured him.

He handed Cindy the blue box.

Jay turned to Cindy. He waved his arms over the box. Over and around and under the box.

Dexter played the drums faster and faster.

Jay took the box back from Cindy. He held it out to Anne. "Do not shudder, do not wince.

This box contains a handsome prince," he announced.

The box flew open and out popped a frog.

Anne jumped.

Jay grabbed the frog and put it back in the box.

"Where did it come from?" asked Anne. "That box was empty. I know it. How did you do it?"

Jay laughed. "It's easy. We have two boxes. This one is just the same size, the same shape, the same weight, the same color. We exchanged it for a dummy box. You were watching Cindy's scarves and listening to Dexter on the drums and looking at me waving my arms, and you didn't notice when we exchanged boxes. This one is a dummy." He motioned to the box that held the frog.

"Wait a minute," said Cindy excitedly. "A dummy, that's it, a dummy!"

"Watch who you're calling a dummy," warned Anne.

Cindy kept talking. "The same size, the same shape, the same color, the same everything!"

"What now?" asked Dexter.

"The book about magic. We can substitute a

dummy. A fake. We can put the paper cover on another book. Terri wouldn't mind—not when it's something so important."

Dexter snapped his fingers. "Perfect! And we can put the fake book where it can be found. Right on the shelf where it belongs. And we can wait and watch. And see who comes for it. Remember, all books are to be returned today. Because the bookmobile is going to be overhauled. So whoever is trying to get the book will expect it to be in the bookmobile and back on the shelf tonight. Someone will come for it."

Cindy spoke quickly. "One of us could hide in the bookmobile closet where Terri hangs her

coat. It's only big enough for one."

"How can we get into the bookmobile?" asked Dexter, picking up the bongo drum.

"With the hidden key. The one in the thinga-majig under the bookmobile," Cindy answered. She glanced at the boys and then at her notebook. "Who should hide?"

"We'll draw straws," said Jay. "And you don't even have to do it if you don't want to. You can stay here."

"Under the bed, I suppose," said Cindy coldly.

"A perfect plan," interrupted Dexter. "We'll go over to the bookmobile as soon as it's dark. We'll put the dummy book on the shelf. One of us will hide in the closet. Two of us will be outside watching and waiting. Ready to come to the rescue if necessary."

"I have no idea what you're talking about," said Anne, looking from one to the other. "But then I never do until afterwards."

"We'll fill you in later," said Cindy. "I guess that's the end of our magic show. But it's not the end of the mystery."

Dexter folded up the sheet, and Cindy put the scarves away.

"It's you kids who make the mysteries," sighed Anne. "When you get to be my age you know everything. Call me if you need me. I'm going back to the kitchen."

"We've got to find a book that's the right size and shape," said Jay. "The same size and shape as the real book."

They quickly scanned the shelves. "Here's one," said Dexter.

Jay and Cindy agreed. In a moment they had put the paper jacket of *Magic, Here, There, and Everywhere* on the dummy book.

"Let's get all the other library books together. The ones we have to take back," said Jay. "Mom's and ours. Whoever is waiting and watching for that one book won't know when it's going to be returned. They'll just know that it will be there sometime today."

Anne walked in from the kitchen. "If you're going to the bookmobile with books anyway, all mine are next to my bed. And don't get sidetracked with your mystery and forget to come home for supper. I'm the chief cook tonight. I'm doing the whole thing as a surprise for Mom."

The detectives gathered the library books together. "These are all the books from this house," said Dexter. "How about all the books at your house?"

"You're sure nobody is waiting over there?" asked Cindy. "The man with the cane or anyone?"

"If you're worried, you can stay here," said Jay impatiently.

"No, I'm coming," said Cindy.

The three hurried next door. The key was in its usual place under the flower pot on the porch.

"All the books are on the hall table," Cindy reminded the boys as they opened the door.

There were no books.

A note was on the table. A note from Mrs. Temple. Jay picked it up. He read it slowly out loud: "Someone called from the library. Said they would pick up all the books for us, isn't that nice? I told them I'd put the books on the porch, since I was just leaving for work. See you later tonight. Don't forget you're having supper with Tates. I'm working late. Love, Mom."

The three detectives stared at the note. Then they stared at each other. "Someone arranged to get the books," said Dexter. "Whoever it was—it was the someone who wanted the *Magic Everywhere* book. Someone who knew Cindy had it."

"Well, they didn't get it," said Jay.

"But they came," said Cindy. "They were right here on the front porch. This morning. What if I'd been here?" She swallowed. "What if I'd been here when they found the magic book wasn't in the pile of books?"

8 · Silent Spy

JAY LOOKED at Cindy. "Well, you *weren't* here," he said sensibly.

"But I might have been when someone came up on our porch. Who was it?" asked Cindy.

"We'll just ask Terri who returned a big pile of books," said Dexter. "That's easy."

"Let's go," said Jay.

The Spotlighters had a quick lunch and gathered up Anne's books.

"I don't see any suspects," Dexter said under his breath as they neared the bookmobile.

"Most of all I don't want to see Dr. Drummond. With his cane," murmured Cindy.

"Let's all go in together," Jay said.

The Spotlighters climbed the steps of the book-mobile and walked in. Terri was there. And Aunt Margaret.

"Welcome back!" Terri exclaimed. "You can just set all those books here on the counter and I'll check them off." She reached for the books.

Suddenly Aunt Margaret leaned across the counter and took the books instead. "I'll mark them off, Terri," she said. "You've been doing all the work today. It's about time I did more of it."

Terri laughed. "Nonsense, Aunt Margaret. You're the hardest-working helper I've ever had."

Cindy stared as Aunt Margaret turned the books over quickly and looked at the spines. Aunt Margaret separated the books in piles. "Any more books?" she asked the Spotlighters, looking around at them.

"These," Dexter said, pushing his armful of books across the counter. "Those are all the books we had out." He looked sideways at Jay, and Jay nodded quickly.

Aunt Margaret looked at the spines and set the books down in separate piles. Then she nodded her head sharply, and her glasses slid off her nose and hung around her neck.

Terri smiled. "I should let you take over the whole bookmobile," she said. "You do everything twice as fast as I do. Even though you had to leave for an hour to take the dog home, you still got more done than I did today."

The Spotlighters exchanged glances. Was this a new clue? Aunt Margaret had left the bookmobile for an hour.

Aunt Margaret chuckled. "It comes from being a librarian for more years than you've been alive, my dear," she said.

"More customers," said Terri as two small boys walked into the bookmobile, their arms filled with books.

"We found these on the sidewalk a couple of blocks from here," said one of the boys.

Cindy stared at the books. "Those are the books Mom and I had," she said. "The ones we were going to bring back. Someone called and offered to pick them up. And someone did."

Cindy glanced at Aunt Margaret. She was putting books on the shelves and seemed to be paying no attention.

"How's the magic show?" she asked when she turned around for more books.

"Fine," said Dexter.

When the Spotlighters were outside, Dexter said, "Did you notice that Aunt Margaret wasn't interested in the books the boys brought in? She didn't touch them." Jay and Cindy nodded.

"And she was gone from the bookmobile for an hour," Cindy said slowly. "She could have picked up the books from our porch and found that the one she wanted was missing. She could have left the books on the sidewalk so no one would know she'd been the one who picked them up."

Jay frowned. "There are at least two people in the mystery," he said. "One is P. Nelson Edward. He made the sign with the message. But there had to be someone who would know how to read it and understand it. Who knew the secret? The secret of the sign? The secret of the red glassses?"

"It could have been Olga," said Cindy. "And she could have asked Aunt Margaret to get the books from our house. Remember that Mom didn't say in her note who called—a man or a woman."

The Spotlighters spent the rest of the afternoon

asking themselves questions about the mystery. Before they knew it, dinner with the Tates was over and it was time to begin their plan. They huddled together on the porch, peering out into the black night.

"Someone may be out there, waiting," whispered Jay.

"We'll have to take a chance," answered Dexter, hugging the dummy book with the *Magic Everywhere* cover closer to him.

"Let's go," said Cindy, taking a last look around. Was Dr. Drummond waiting out there? With his cane? She shivered.

The three Spotlighters slipped from the porch and walked quickly down the street. Cindy glanced behind her. "Let's hurry," she said.

They quickened their pace and were silent until they reached the darkened shops and the bookmobile. Quickly they slid behind the Happy Cleaners small van. It was parked only a few yards from the bookmobile.

"Everything seems so empty," Cindy whispered, looking at the closed shops. "It's like a sleeping town. Bewitched, like Sleeping Beauty's castle."

They peered ahead at the bookmobile.

"No one's come yet," said Dexter, pushing his glasses down on his nose.

"Or else whoever it is has already come and gone," Jay frowned.

"No, I think it's too early," argued Dexter. "The skylight is closed. If anyone was in there, they'd have left it open for a quick getaway."

Cindy nodded. "Dexter's right. I think we're the first ones here. But let's hurry and draw straws before I get cold feet. I want to get it over."

Quickly Jay looked around on the ground. He found three twigs. They were all different lengths. He held his closed fist out.

"Here," he said. "Shortest twig wins."

"Or loses, you mean," whispered Dexter.

Cindy drew first and waited until the boys had each chosen a twig. They faced each other.

"Ready?" whispered Cindy.

"Ready," the boys whispered back.

They opened their palms. Cindy had drawn the shortest twig.

Jay said quickly, "We can draw again if you want."

Cindy shook her head. "Don't be silly."

They looked around once more, and headed toward the bookmobile.

Dexter nudged Cindy. "Here's the book, the dummy one. I'll go get the key." He stole quietly to the other side of the bookmobile. Jay and Cindy waited at the bottom of the steps, their hearts pounding.

"I can't find the key," whispered Dexter. Cindy and Jay looked at each other in the dark.

"Wait," said Dexter. "Here it is." In a moment he was at their side. "I'll unlock the door and put the key back. You can always open the door from the inside without the key."

"In you go, Cindy," said Jay. "And don't worry. If we hear anything, we'll save you."

"Come if I scream or anything," said Cindy faintly.

"Right," Jay nodded. He patted Cindy's arm.

Cindy shivered and stepped through the door. The bookmobile had an empty feel. Not a sound! It was pitch black inside. "I can't see a thing," she whispered, reaching for her flashlight.

"Ready?" Dexter asked her.

She nodded and patted the dummy book under

her arm. "I'm all set." She took a deep breath and closed the door quietly. She heard muffled sounds as the boys climbed down the steps. She kept her ear pressed to the door until the sound faded away.

She flicked on her flashlight for a moment and moved it quickly around the bookmobile. Yes, everything looked in place. Then she stepped quietly over to the shelves where the missing book belonged. She slid the dummy book into place. Then she stood back to take a look. No one would be able to tell the difference, she told herself. Not until later.

Cindy turned her flashlight to the closet door and walked over to it. She reached for the handle. Then suddenly she pulled her hand back.

What if someone was hiding in the closet? Someone who had heard them talking, someone who had heard her come into the bookmobile, someone who might be listening to her even now? Suddenly she was afraid.

She swallowed and quickly pulled open the closet door. A shapeless figure stood waiting. She gasped—and then realized it was a patchwork raincoat of Terri's, hanging on a hook. She breathed a sigh of relief. Her heart was still pounding.

Cindy closed the closet door behind her. She tried to get used to the dark. There was no sound.

Carefully she pushed the closet door open a tiny crack. She'd have to be able to see who it was. Anyone coming in would not notice the slit in the door. She hoped.

Cindy waited. And waited.

What about the boys? Had someone sneaked up and discovered them waiting? Cindy thought of Dr. Drummond's heavy silver cane and shivered.

Suddenly there was the sound of a car motor. She held her breath. She heard a muffled conversation. She heard a car door close quietly. The motor kept running. She could hear her own heart pounding in the dark closet.

A minute passed. Cindy kept her ear pressed against the closet door. Suddenly she drew back. She heard a different noise this time. Something much closer. She strained to hear more.

It was a scraping noise. Very close. Something was scraping against the bookmobile. And then almost at once she heard a step.

A man's voice said, "All right, you go in. I'll wait in the car."

Cindy held her breath. The key! Someone had just taken it from its secret place, hidden under the bookmobile.

But who could it be? Maybe it was Terri, coming back because she had forgotten something. Maybe she had a date. Cindy breathed in relief. It had to be Terri. And how would Cindy explain what she was doing in the closet? She almost giggled. Poor Terri would be frightened half out of her wits!

The door of the bookmobile opened. And then closed, quietly.

Cindy took a deep breath. Terri would be flicking on the overhead light. Cindy was ready. She didn't want to frighten Terri. She'd just say, "Hey, Terri, it's me, Cindy."

Footsteps moved closer. And then through the crack in the door Cindy saw the sudden glow of a flashlight.

But Terri wouldn't use a flashlight, she'd turn on the lights.

Cindy leaned closer to the crack in the closet door. The bright light moved inside the bookmobile. Suddenly Cindy jumped. There was a series of thumps. What was it?

Someone was throwing books on the floor! The ones on the counter—the ones Terri hadn't put back on the shelves.

Then it wasn't Terri. It couldn't be. Cindy's heart pounded so loudly she was sure whoever it was would hear.

The footsteps moved away, and Cindy could see the flashlight moving along the row of books where she had put the dummy book. And then Cindy saw a hand stretch out and move along the shelf.

Cindy caught her breath. She recognized a golden ring, a ring in the shape of a serpent with a red eye.

Olga Ratchett!

And then without any warning Cindy felt an enormous thump. The bookmobile shook, and Cindy reeled against the closet wall. Someone must have jumped down through the skylight window.

There was a scream. Cindy wondered if she had screamed. Or if she hadn't, maybe Olga Ratchett had. And then a familiar voice said, "All right now, give me that book."

Cindy's head swam. The voice was the voice of P. Nelson Edward.

9 · Start Talking!

CINDY PEERED through the crack of the closet door.

Olga Ratchett had dropped her flashlight. It cast an eerie glow in the bookmobile. Cindy could see the dim shapes of P. Nelson and Olga Ratchett struggling for the book. Suddenly P. Nelson held it high over his head.

"Give that back!" cried Olga Ratchett.

"Not on your life," said P. Nelson.

"I trusted you!" cried Olga Ratchett. "I trusted you. You can't take it from me!"

She lunged toward P. Nelson, her long fingers reaching for his face.

Cindy leaned closer to see. And suddenly she lost her balance! She fell out of the closet with a thud.

Then everything happened at once. There was a quick gasp as Olga Ratchett wheeled around. Olga grabbed the book from P. Nelson and hugged it to her. Before Cindy had a chance to get up, P. Nelson shouted, "Give it to me!"

Then the bookmobile door slammed. Olga Ratchett was gone. She was gone, and she had the book. Cindy heard her running down the steps. "Let's go!" Olga called to someone.

P. Nelson sprang to the door and threw it open. He jumped down the steps. A car door slammed. Cindy could hear the car pulling away and P. Nelson running after it.

Then in a moment he was back.

Suddenly the lights in the bookmobile blinded her. Cindy blinked and lifted her head. She stared into the blazing eyes of P. Nelson Edward.

Her heart pounded. What would he do to her?

At that moment there was a loud thumping on the roof. The skylight window was thrown open. A dark figure jumped down, narrowly missing P. Nelson. And then another. Jay and Dexter! Cindy trembled in relief.

"You're safe, Cindy!" shouted Jay.

"Don't worry, we're here!" Dexter added.

Cindy was shaking. She tried to stand up.

P. Nelson looked at her angrily. He ran his fingers through his curly red hair.

"You ruined it, you ruined it," he said in a low voice. "Olga got the book because of you. I had it, but when you fell out of the closet I was startled. She had a chance to grab it back. Now she's gone and she's got the book. Am I in trouble! Real trouble."

"Suppose you tell us everything," said Cindy severely. She was no longer afraid.

P. Nelson hesitated. "I don't know where to begin."

"At the beginning," said Dexter firmly.

Then suddenly there was the sound of a motor coming closer.

"Olga Ratchett's coming back!" said Jay.

"No, that's a motorbike," said Dexter, cocking his head and listening.

"It's Terri," said Cindy. She threw open the bookmobile door. "Terri! We're in here! Hurry!"

Terri pulled up. She turned off the motor and pushed down the kickstand. Then she started toward them, taking off her helmet.

"What on earth?" she asked, when she saw them standing in the bookmobile with P. Nelson. "What are all of you doing here? I called your mother and she said you'd left a note that you were here. Why? Just as I was coming I saw Olga Ratchett drive off with a bald head. Not Olga with a bald head! A man with a bald head."

"A bald head," said P. Nelson glumly. "That will be Gus Garvy."

The Spotlighters looked at each other. Who was Gus Garvy?

"What are you all doing here?" repeated Terri. "How did you get in? What's going on?"

"Come on in, Terri," said Jay. "P. Nelson was just going to explain, weren't you?"

P. Nelson looked at Terri and at the three Spotlighters. "I was just thinking how I was going to tell you everything. It's a very complicated story."

"Start," said Cindy, opening her notebook.

"It all began with Olga Ratchett. I used to see her in a chemistry class. It was before I'd met Terri or you kids. Before I'd heard of Dr. Drummond."

"You lied to us," said Cindy. "You said you

didn't know Dr. Drummond. Or Olga."

P. Nelson nodded miserably. "Yes, I lied to you. But I won't lie any more. I promise. What I'm going to tell you is the truth, the whole truth, and nothing but the truth."

"Good," said Dexter, pushing his glasses down on his nose.

P. Nelson scratched his ear. "This is what really happened. I got to know Olga Ratchett. She knew a man named Gus Garvy."

"The baldheaded man," said Cindy.

"Gus Garvy owns a company that makes plastics. He had heard of the new plastic that Dr. Drummond was experimenting with. He tried to get Dr. Drummond to sell him some of his chemical formulas for this new plastic. He told Dr. Drummond it would mean a lot of money to both of them. But Dr. Drummond turned Gus Garvy down."

"Why?" asked Dexter.

"Because he knew Gus Garvy would use the new plastic for something wrong."

"What do you mean, something wrong?" asked Jay.

"I don't know. Something about toys. Toys

that would be dangerous. Anyway, Dr. Drummond wouldn't sell Gus Garvy the formula. So Garvy decided to steal it."

"Steal," murmured Cindy.

"But where does Olga Ratchett come in?" asked Jay.

"Gus Garvy asked Olga to get a job with Dr. Drummond, who needed a good secretary. And Olga's a good secretary. So Drummond hired her."

"Who wouldn't hire an Olga?" asked Terri.

P. Nelson glanced at Terri.

"Olga began to watch for all Dr. Drummond's formulas for plastics. She really knows a lot about chemistry, so it wasn't hard for her. Of course Dr.

Drummond was happy to have such a good secretary. He didn't suspect what she was doing."

"What *was* she doing?" asked Cindy, writing.

"Olga was making copies of some of his work and giving them to Gus Garvy," said P. Nelson. "He was buying the copies of Dr. Drummond's work from her."

"She was stealing the formulas from Dr. Drummond to give to Garvy," said Jay, nodding. "But how are you involved in all this?"

"I'm getting to that," said P. Nelson. "Dr. Drummond found out about it. I don't know how. But he fired Olga Ratchett. And he hired a new secretary, one who didn't know anything about chemistry or plastics."

"Virginia Pipestone," said Dexter.

P. Nelson looked over with raised eyebrows.

"I followed Dr. Drummond," explained Dexter. "I found out where he lived. And then I found out who he was."

"I see," said P. Nelson. "You're quite a team of detectives." He cleared his throat.

"Go on," said Dexter. "Just how did you get involved with Dr. Drummond?"

"Well, Dr. Drummond found his new secretary, Virginia Pipestone, couldn't do all the special typing. All those chemical formulas and figures are hard to do. He had to have his work finished by a certain date. So he put up a notice on the university bulletin board in the chemistry building. He wanted an expert typist."

P. Nelson stopped and glanced around at the detectives and Terri. "I'm an expert typist," he declared modestly. "Of chemical information."

Cindy wrote that in her notebook. She added, "And an expert liar."

"Olga Ratchett saw the notice," P. Nelson went on. "She knew I was looking for a job. I'm working my way through graduate school—in chemistry, you know. And I'm always looking for jobs." He sighed and ran his fingers through his curly red hair. "Well, Olga took the notice down before anyone else had a chance to answer it. Olga called me. We made an appointment to see each other for lunch."

"That's not an appointment," said Terri. "That's a date."

P. Nelson looked at the floor. "Of course Olga is beautiful. But being beautiful isn't everything."

"It beats whatever comes second," said Terri, her cheeks red.

P. Nelson glanced up and then looked down at his shoes. "Anyway, she told me about the job with Dr. Drummond. I hadn't seen the notice. And I needed a job. Olga told me some lies. I believed her." He stared miserably at the circle of faces.

"What lies?" demanded Cindy, turning a page in her notebook.

"She told me Dr. Drummond had cheated Gus Garvy. She said Dr. Drummond had taken money from Garvy and then given him phony plans, ones that wouldn't work. She told me she had helped Gus Garvy by giving him copies of Drummond's work. She was really stealing Dr. Drummond's work, but of course she didn't call it that. She made it sound as if Gus Garvy was getting what he had been cheated out of by Dr. Drummond."

"And you believed her?" asked Jay.

P. Nelson nodded.

Terri sniffed. "As you say, she *is* beautiful."

"She must have been afraid I would learn she was fired. So she told me some story about Dr. Drummond finding out that she was a friend of Gus Garvy and firing her because of that. Which is probably true. He must have seen Olga and Garvy together. And *that* made him suspect Olga was on Garvy's side. Anyway, all I knew was that I had a job with Dr. Drummond, and I was glad of that."

"But what happened?" asked Cindy.

"After I got the job, Olga asked me to give her copies of Dr. Drummond's work. I was to copy the formulas, the way she had done when she worked for him. I thought I was doing the right thing. I thought Gus Garvy deserved to have them because Dr. Drummond had cheated him and kept Garvy's money."

He looked at Terri. "It's hard now to understand how I could have believed her. But I did."

"So you gave her copies of Dr. Drummond's work?" asked Cindy, writing in her notebook.

P. Nelson nodded. "But she told me she didn't want either of us to get into any trouble. So I was to give copies of Dr. Drummond's papers to her secretly."

"Secretly," repeated Cindy, nodding.

"Yes, in a secret code. Each time I would use a different library book from the bookmobile. I hid each message in a different book."

"Why all the secrecy?" asked Jay.

"Olga thought that if Dr. Drummond saw us together, he would suspect I was giving her the information she had tried to get herself. For Gus Garvy. She didn't want us to be seen together at all. Not by Dr. Drummond. Not by anyone. Aunt Margaret knew Dr. Drummond because she used to work in the university library. If she had seen us together, Aunt Margaret might have mentioned it to Dr. Drummond."

P. Nelson sighed. "It's all so complicated."

"Everything gets complicated when you get tangled up with a complicated woman," said Terri. "One who uses other people."

P. Nelson tried a smile, but Terri did not smile back. He went on. "Anyway, we couldn't even use the telephone because Aunt Margaret might answer. Olga has been living at Aunt Margaret's for a couple of months. Well, we worked out a system of secret messages."

"Go on," said Cindy, still writing busily.

"I would take out a book at the bookmobile. I'd use it to hold the message—the information Olga wanted."

"And I thought you were such a great reader," said Terri bitterly. "Interested in so many subjects."

"I am," said P. Nelson. "Anyway I'd return the book to the bookmobile, with the hidden message. Then I'd put the book's catalog number somewhere in the sign. I really worked hard on those signs. Well, then Olga would come after I'd finished the sign and read it. Then she'd know which book to get at the bookmobile."

"But how could she read the code?" asked Cindy. "I never saw her with any special glasses."

"Remember that pendant she has? It's shaped like an eye. With a red jewel in the center. It's really red glass. She looked through that."

"So that was it!" exclaimed Cindy.

P. Nelson nodded. "Olga always came after I was gone. We planned it that way. I was never to be there when she came."

"And she came at three o'clock," said Cindy, glancing at her notebook. "You were never there when she came—until yesterday. You were still there, and was she angry!"

"Yes," said P. Nelson. "I promised her I'd never be there after two o'clock."

"Why were you there yesterday?" asked Jay. "What happened?"

"Well, yesterday morning I found my job with Dr. Drummond was over. Virginia Pipestone told me. All I needed to do was file some papers and mail some letters in the afternoon. It really wasn't such a great job. I was just a typist and an errand boy. But I wanted Terri to think it was important."

He looked at Terri, but she glanced away.

"Anyway, I knew that if my job was over, there would be no more information for Olga. So the message I had put in the magic book was the last one. And it was the most important one. It had the final formulas for the new plastic. I had to let Olga know. So I came back to add the words 'Last One' to the sign."

"And that's when Olga found you there," said Cindy. "She really was mad."

He nodded. "She has a temper. And then I went back to Dr. Drummond's. And that's when I found out the truth. The truth about Olga Ratchett."

10 · Very Convincing, But–

P. NELSON REACHED into his pocket. "There was this letter. This is a carbon. It's addressed to a chemistry professor at another university. I mailed the original. Listen—"

Dear Henry:

Here is the manuscript for my article on a new type of plastic. It has taken some time to work this out. And it was very nearly stolen from me! Would you believe that anyone would do that?

I would not sell my formulas to Gus Garvy. He owns Picky Plastics, you know. He wanted to use my plastic to make toys that wouldn't have been safe.

Garvy was angry when I wouldn't sell him my formula. So he persuaded my secretary to copy my work and give it to him. I caught on to what she was doing and fired her. So the new plastics formula is safe. And here it is for you to test.

And now my vacation. My grandchildren are coming for a week's visit, and then we're all going off to the woods, fishing and all that.

Dave

P. Nelson looked around again at the three detectives and Terri. "So I knew Dr. Drummond was on the level. He was not the crook at all. Olga was the crook—stealing and getting me to do it, too." He shook his head miserably. "And it's serious for me. Very serious. Dr. Drummond could accuse me of stealing his work. It would ruin my career."

Dexter cleared his throat. "All of a sudden you found out what Olga was doing. Why didn't you go and tell Dr. Drummond what you knew?"

"Because I thought I could get that book back, the book with the last message. Without that formula, nothing else would work. No one could make the new plastic but Dr. Drummond."

Cindy looked up at Jay and then back at her notes.

P. Nelson went on, "So last night I broke into the bookmobile through the skylight. The book was gone! Had Olga beaten me to it? When? Where was the book if she hadn't taken it? I knew the bookmobile was closed when she came yesterday. I was there when Terri closed early. It never occurred to me that anyone else could have checked the book out before that. I'd make a poor detective."

Cindy nodded.

"Anyway, I knew I had to do something. If Olga got the book, she'd give the formula to Gus Garvy. I had to persuade her not to. I couldn't sleep last night, I was so worried. First thing this morning I went to her house. I waited outside until I saw her leave with her dog. I ran over to her and asked her to listen to me. I told her I knew she had lied to me. I knew she and Garvy were stealing from Dr. Drummond. I told her I had learned that Dr. Drummond had not cheated Garvy."

"What did she say?" Jay asked.

"Olga was so angry she would have screamed

at me—but there were people around. She accused me of hiding the book with the last formula! Then I knew she didn't have the book after all. But she said she knew who had the book. She was going to get that book, no matter what she had to do."

Cindy shivered. So it was Olga who knew Cindy had the book.

"I tried to follow Olga. You know, shadow her. But I'm not very good at being a detective. She walked down the alley behind Random Street."

Cindy nudged Jay.

"I kept out of sight behind Olga. Later she came back to Random Street and picked up some books from someone's front porch. I thought maybe the special book was in the pile. But I watched her. She looked at all the books. Then she left them on a corner. So I knew she still didn't have the book. But she knew who had it. And I didn't."

P. Nelson clenched his fist and pounded it into his other hand. "If only I hadn't gotten mixed up with Olga Ratchett!" he said.

Cindy glanced at Terri. Terri smiled and winked.

"Well, Olga went back to her house. And she

didn't come out. I waited and waited for hours. Finally I realized she had tricked me. She had left the house by another door and sneaked away. She must have seen me following her. I'm no detective."

"What did you do then?" asked Cindy.

"What could I do? Nothing. I didn't know where Olga was. And I didn't know who had the book. Then I remembered that every book had to be returned to the bookmobile today. Maybe the book was there now. I decided to go to the bookmobile after dark. Just as I had last night. I was going to climb in through the skylight."

"But you didn't?" asked Jay.

P. Nelson shook his head. "I heard a car coming. I hid and watched. It was Olga, and Gus Garvy was with her."

"That must have been just after I got into the bookmobile and hid in the closet," said Cindy.

P. Nelson continued, "I watched. Gus Garvy waited in the car. Olga reached under the bookmobile and found the hidden key. I don't know how she knew it was there."

"She probably saw me take it out sometime," said Terri. "I've forgotten my key a couple of times this week and had to use that one."

"I realized that Olga still hadn't found the book. She meant to look for it. So it was in the bookmobile after all! I decided to jump in through the skylight and surprise her."

Pounding his fist in his hand, P. Nelson said, "It worked. I surprised her. I had the book. But now she's got it. She's got the book, and she's got the formula. And now I'm in real trouble."

"Well, don't worry," said Dexter, pushing his glasses up on his head. "The book—"

Darting an angry glance at Dexter, Cindy interrupted. "He has every reason to worry. After all, if Olga has the book, Gus Garvy has the formula. It's too late." Cindy turned toward Jay and winked meaningfully.

"Yes, it's too late," said P. Nelson. "Dr. Drummond's work is all for nothing. And it's all my fault. I'm in disgrace. Maybe I'll even go to jail."

Cindy tapped her notebook. "Your story is very, very convincing, P. Nelson Edward," she said severely. "Except for one thing."

"What's that?" he asked, frowning.

The boys looked at Cindy, puzzled. She said,

"You've been working for Dr. Drummond the past few weeks." P. Nelson nodded. "At his house," Cindy continued. Another nod.

"But Dr. David Drummond had never seen you until yesterday afternoon. So you've lied to us once more, haven't you? You never worked for him at all."

Dexter, Jay and Terri all stared at P. Nelson and waited for his answer. Had he been lying to them again? What was going on?

"I can explain," he said quickly. "I really never met Dr. Drummond. I worked for him, but I never saw him. He was gone by the time I came to work. And I left before he returned. My only contact was Virginia Pipestone. She hired me. She gave me the things to type."

He glanced around at the Spotlighters and at Terri. "You've got to believe me," he said earnestly.

Cindy looked at her watch. "It's late. Mom is going to be worried. Let's go back to the house and finish our talk."

"Right," said P. Nelson eagerly, looking around at the crowded bookshelves. "Let's get out of here."

They went outside, and Terri locked the bookmobile behind them.

Suddenly P. Nelson wheeled around and faced the Spotlighters and Terri. "Listen!" he said. "It's a car. A sports car! It's Olga—coming back. What for?"

Olga's car screeched to a stop not far from the bookmobile. She jumped out and slammed the car door.

Terri whispered, "That man isn't with her. The one I saw her with when she left. Gus Garvy. She's alone."

Cindy spoke quickly. "There's only one way to prove you're telling the truth, P. Nelson. We'll hide behind the bookmobile. And we'll listen to you and Olga. Then we'll know."

The three detectives and Terri ducked behind the bookmobile.

Everything happened quickly. Olga Ratchett ran toward the bookmobile as P. Nelson stepped out of the shadows.

"You're back, Olga," he said.

She jumped when she saw him. "It's a fake!" she said. "You tricked me! I'll get you for this!"

"What do you mean?" asked P. Nelson.

Suddenly Olga Ratchett's voice changed. Slowly, softly, she said, "You didn't know, did you? Of course you didn't. You wouldn't have struggled with me if you'd known it was a fake. Listen. We've been tricked. Both of us. The book was a dummy."

"A dummy?" asked P. Nelson.

"It's those kids," said Olga Ratchett. "It's got to be. Those two boys and that girl, that awful girl. I'll get her if it's the last thing I do. And they're probably working with that dumb librarian."

"Look," said Olga, her voice soft and coaxing now. "I know that girl has the real book, the one with the last formula in it. She must have it. And they tricked us. They put the right cover on another book to fool us. But we'll get the real book back somehow."

P. Nelson was silent.

"We've got to get that book," said Olga slowly. "You can help me. And then Gus Garvy will have David Drummond's invention, all of it."

And still P. Nelson stood there, silent.

"What's the matter with you?" Olga asked sharply. Then her voice became soft again. "Look, if you help me get that book, I'll split the money with you, fifty-fifty. You'll get half of what Gus Garvy gives me. And that's a lot of money, honey. All you have to do is get that book from the girl. I don't care how you do it. If you have to frighten her into it, fine. If you have to twist her arm, fine. Just get the book."

"Did you hear that, Cindy?" P. Nelson asked in a loud voice.

Olga gasped.

11 · Abracadabra

WITH WIDE EYES, Cindy walked with Terri and the boys to the front of the bookmobile.

"Why you little—" Olga Ratchett lunged toward Cindy. Her long, pointed fingernails almost touched Cindy's face. Cindy covered her face with her hands.

P. Nelson grabbed Olga by the arm and pulled her back. Olga Ratchett struggled to get away from his grip.

"You're through, Olga," P. Nelson said through clenched teeth. "You're through lying and stealing and cheating!"

Olga Ratchett tried to jerk her arm away. "Let go of me, you fool! You're hurting me."

P. Nelson loosened his grip on her arm, but he didn't let go.

"Ha!" Olga breathed. "You say I'm through! With this town, yes. I'm getting as far away from this place as I can."

She glared at Cindy. "If it hadn't been for you and those nosey boys . . ."

Cindy swallowed and said nothing.

"You can let go of me now," Olga said. "I'm getting out of here. No one from this dumb town will ever see me again."

P. Nelson let go of Olga Ratchett. She spun around and ran toward her car. Just as she was driving off, she rolled down her car window. The Spotlighters watched as she leaned her head out of the window and shouted, "Fools! All of you, fools!"

Her tires squealed as she sped off.

Cindy turned to P. Nelson. "I'm sorry I didn't believe you, but I had to be sure. Mr. Hooley's Rule. And then we have another rule, the Usher Rule. It says you have to suspect people—even if you like them. So I had to suspect you. That's what being a detective is all about."

P. Nelson nodded. "I know. That's all right.

And now you all know everything."

He turned to Terri. "You probably won't have anything to do with me after this. Now that you know I was stealing Dr. Drummond's secrets."

Terri smiled. "Who knows?" she said.

Half an hour later they were all sitting in the Temple living room. Mrs. Temple was curled up in her favorite chair.

Cindy tapped her notebook with her pencil. "There are still some unanswered questions, I think. Like why was Dr. Drummond so mad at Olga yesterday? And what did he write down about the bookmobile?"

P. Nelson swallowed. "I'll find out. I'm going over to his house first thing in the morning and I'm going to tell him everything."

"Last night when we came over to the bookmobile someone was in it. With matches. That was you, wasn't it?" asked Jay.

P. Nelson nodded. "I'd forgotten a flashlight—I'm not a very good detective. Anyway, I did have matches in my pocket."

"Had you gone to the wedding?" asked Cindy.

"No, but Dr. Drummond had, and there were

lots of matchbooks in his office at home. The matches weren't much good in the bookmobile. Anyway I couldn't find the book and so I left."

"What happened after that?" asked Jay. "When we went in the next morning we found out someone had been there again."

"Olga," said P. Nelson. "She must have come back for the book after I left. She got in with the key from that magnetic holder, I guess."

"Then it was Olga who left Dr. Drummond's silver pen," said Cindy. "And Olga who wrote my name down. When the book wasn't there, she looked in the card file of borrowers to see if anyone had taken it out."

"That's what I should have done," said P. Nelson. "Then we'd never have had all this excitement."

"And she was the one who called Mom about the books," said Jay.

"Yes," said Cindy. "Now I remember telling Olga that we were coming early—right after breakfast with Mom, before she left for work. So Olga knew we'd be at the bookmobile and she called before Mom left for work. She knew Mom would believe it was the library calling. Mom left the books on the porch for her, and Olga picked them up. When she saw the book she wanted wasn't there, she left them all on the sidewalk."

Cindy licked the tip of her pencil. "I wonder if Aunt Margaret really *was* spying for Olga Ratchett. Trying to find that book."

"I doubt it," Terri said. "She didn't look at half the books that were brought in. She was just very helpful and friendly."

"We still have one important question, P. Nelson," said Cindy. "Wait a minute." She ran upstairs. In a moment she was back with the book that Olga had wanted so much. "Here's the book. But where is the message?"

P. Nelson laughed. He took the book and opened it wide. Then he took out a little penknife. He carefully ran it between the spine of the book and the binding. There was a narrow space there. He shook the book, and out fell a paper folded to fit into the spine of the book. It had been held by a little tape.

"Here you are," said P. Nelson. And he unfolded the paper to show that it was covered with figures and directions. "Gus Garvy can't make the new plastic without this," he said, putting it into his pocket. "I'll have to tell Dr. Drummond everything tomorrow. How I dread it. I won't sleep a wink."

"Why not tonight?" asked Terri. "It's not too late."

"The telephone's right in the hall," said Cindy.

P. Nelson groaned. But he walked into the hall. They couldn't help listening.

"Hello, Dr. Drummond? I hope I'm not calling too late. This is P. Nelson Edward. Yes, I've been working for you." He paused and Cindy could hear him swallowing. "Could I come over to see you for a moment? It's very important. Thank you. I'll be right over."

P. Nelson walked back into the room. "For better or for worse, I'm seeing him," he announced.

"You can borrow my motorbike," said Terri. "We'll wait here for you."

Terri handed P. Nelson her helmet. He put it on and waved goodbye to everyone in the room. They listened to the sound of the motorbike until it was out of earshot.

"What if Dr. Drummond is angry with P. Nelson?" worried Cindy. "What if he calls the police?"

"It's still better to get it over with," said Jay.

"I'm glad it's not me," said Dexter. "If I were Dr. Drummond, I'd be really angry to find out someone was copying my work and giving it to an enemy."

"Yes, but P. Nelson didn't know what he was doing," said Cindy.

"*I* knew," said Terri smugly. "I knew all along she was an evil woman. You can't trust anyone who's that beautiful."

Mrs. Temple smiled. "It's exciting to be in on

one of your mysteries. Even if I'm only coming in at the end of it."

They were just finishing the story for Mrs. Temple when they heard the sound of Terri's motorbike.

"That was fast," said Terri. "I wonder—" She went to the door. Dr. Drummond and a smiling P. Nelson Edward were just coming up the porch steps.

"I always wanted to ride on one of those things," said Dr. Drummond, his eyes twinkling. "And I've always been interested in magic. And in mysteries. And this young man tells me I'll find a little of both over here tonight."

In a few minutes they were all sitting around the dining room table over hot chocolate: the three detectives, Mrs. Temple, Terri Firestone, P. Nelson Edward, and Dr. Drummond. Cindy had her notebook open and ready.

The Spotlighters quickly explained their part in the mystery to Dr. Drummond.

"I see, I see," he nodded. "Let me say that I do not hold this young man responsible for what he has done—or tried to do. He sincerely believed Olga Ratchett when she told him I had stolen secrets from

Gus Garvy. Of course he thought *I* was the villain."

"And it was Olga Ratchett. And Gus Garvy," said Dexter.

"What about Aunt Margaret?" asked Jay. "Was she helping Olga Ratchett?"

"Not at all," said Dr. Drummond. "She was not very fond of her niece. In fact, I believe she will be relieved to discover that Olga Ratchett is leaving town for good. Olga is not an easy person to get along with. She's very selfish. And she has a wicked temper and a quick tongue."

P. Nelson nodded.

"Let me explain," said Dr. Drummond. "Olga was working for me. And I saw Olga and Gus Garvy in a restaurant in Chicago. That was a shock. I began to suspect they were in a plot together. A plot to steal my chemical formulas for the special plastic. And to use it for toys that would be dangerous."

"What do you mean?" asked Jay.

"My new plastic is very cheap. Very durable. But it has to be used under special conditions. Controlled conditions. Gus Garvy wanted to make chilren's toys with it."

"What's wrong with that?" asked Cindy.

"Because when the plastic is exposed to high temperatures it melts and gives off poisonous fumes. A child could leave a toy under a steam radiator, for instance."

"I see," said Cindy, nodding and writing in her notebook.

"I suspected Olga when I saw her with Gus Garvy. So I laid a trap," said Dr. Drummond, glancing around the table.

"A trap?" asked Cindy, looking up from her notebook.

"I gave Olga Ratchett some false formulas to type. I knew that if she copied them and gave them to Gus Garvy he would know they were false. I waited and watched. And a few days later Olga came to me and asked me if there had been some mistake in the formulas! I knew then. When I asked her, she confessed. I fired her. She promised never to see Gus Garvy again. And I hired a new secretary."

"But when we saw you, you were angry with her," Cindy reminded him.

"Yes, I was very angry. Because she was still seeing Gus Garvy. That meant they were trying to work out some scheme to get the formulas."

Cindy glanced once again at her notebook. "I think we've covered almost everything," she said. "But what were you writing down yesterday? Was it something about the bookmobile? Or the sign?"

Dr. Drummond turned to Cindy. "You are indeed very observant detectives," he said admiringly. "I was copying the times for the magic show. I wanted to bring my grandchildren."

"There won't be a magic show if you Spotlighters don't get some sleep," said Mrs. Temple.

"Right," said Cindy, closing her notebook. "That's the end of *that* mystery. I'm all notebooked out."

The magic show the next day was a huge success. Everyone was there. "Everyone except Olga Ratchett," said Cindy, glancing around at the crowd after the show was over.

Aunt Margaret bustled up. "Olga moved out. Took her dog. I have to say I'm very glad she's gone."

"Time to get the bookmobile to the repair shop," Terri announced as she climbed in. "Off I go."

Dr. Drummond and his grandchildren watched.

"Is the library going away?" his grandson asked. "Is it going to disappear?"

Cindy nodded. "Just say the magic word."

The boy thought for a moment. "Fee-fi-fo-fum," he said.

"That's a giant word, not a magic word," Cindy told him. "Try Abracadabra!"

"Abracadabra!" called the boy, waving his arms.

Terri grinned, and the bookmobile started to move. "A bewitched bookmobile," she called. "See you all next week!"

"Beautiful," said P. Nelson under his breath.

"Terri?" asked Cindy.

"No, the bookmobile," said P. Nelson. "Terri—Terri's fantastic. And to think it took me all this time to figure that out! As I keep telling you, I'm not a very good detective."